This book is for E

For information address Hyperion Books for Children,
114 Fifth Avenue, New York, New York 10011-5690.

First Edition
1 3 5 7 9 10 8 6 4 2
Printed in Singapore

Library of Congress Cataloging-in-Publication Data
Raschka, Christopher.
Doggy Dog / by Chris Raschka.—1st ed.
p. cm.—(Thingy things)
Summary: Simple words and illustrations detail some
of the things that Doggy Dog is not,
including a cat, a lampshade, and a potato.
ISBN 0-7868-0642-7 (trade)
[1.Dogs—Fiction.] I. Title.
PZ7.R1814 Do   2000
[E]—dc21   99-51777

Visit www.hyperionchildrensbooks.com

THINGY THINGS
Doggy Dog

Chris Raschka

HYPERION BOOKS FOR CHILDREN
NEW YORK

Doggy Dog,
you are a dog.

You are no cat.

You are no lampshade.

Doggy Dog,
you are not
a footstool.

You are not
a potato.

Doggy Dog,
are you a big cheese?

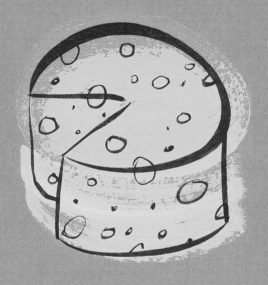

No!

Doggy Dog,
you are a dog!